THE MATING SEASON

by

Allan Banford

Table of Contents

Chapter I

Crandon

THE SUN EMERGED OVER the gleaming skyscrapers of Crandon, bathing the futuristic metropolis in a warm golden glow. Crandon was a city of order, efficiency, and purpose, where every aspect of life was meticulously controlled. Through the orderly bustling streets, we observed the citizens beginning their day with robotic precision, following the same routines day after day in complete harmony.

We meet Jona, a young administrative clerk. She begins her day with practiced efficiency in her compact apartment, ingesting a series of nutrient pills specifically formulated by the government for optimum productivity.

After closing the sleek sleeping pod that all Crandon citizens use for strictly optimized and efficient sleep, she makes her way to work.

Upon arriving at the large government building, Jona immediately joins her colleagues in discussing the latest decrees handed down regarding mating cycles and genetically ideal pair assignments. "Did you hear about the new ovulation regulations?" Jona casually mentions to her friend Remi, who works beside her as a fellow administrative clerk. Remi rolls his eyes in response, playfully exasperated by the government's constant micromanaging of reproduction.

The two spend the day processing paperwork, analyzing statistics, and filing reports, contributing to the smooth bureaucratic workings of the city. Everything is perfectly controlled and scheduled, with no problems or unpredictability. At the end of the strictly regimented workday, Jona and Remi part ways, heading back to their government-assigned living quarters to follow the pre-planned routine until the next workday.

Remi smirked in response to Jona's comment about the latest reproductive decree, quipping that it seemed like the government was trying to micromanage every detail of their love lives. Jona chuckled lightly in agreement - at least all the rules kept things interesting. In Crandon, reproduction was viewed not as a matter of personal choice, but as a civic duty.

Inside the sterile government office, Jona worked diligently at her desk, though her thoughts occasionally drifted to the upcoming Summit of Ministries, the final bureaucratic step in Crandon's highly-engineered reproductive process. Every detail was planned out months in advance to ensure the success of the mating cycle.

As the day progressed, Jona felt the familiar lifeless lull of ... eriod settling in. For now, life plodded on in its ... lerly fashion, just as intended by Crandon's

Later, during their break in the cafeteria, Jona and Remi sat together watching a lone aircraft pass by through the window. Jona pointed out the plane, remarking on how surreal it seemed, a rare sight of individualism against Crandon's perfectly uniform backdrop. Remi smirked and commented that perhaps it was a sign - a sign that things in their overly-controlled city were about to change. Jona laughed at her friend's fanciful notion and dismissed it, returning to eat her strictly nutritious, government-formulated meal.

Little did the two young clerks know, but Crandon's calm facade was indeed about to be shattered...

Eight months passed. The city buzzed with activity as preparations for the upcoming highly-regulated mating season were underway. Every minute detail had been planned out months in advance to ensure the cycle's success.

Inside the government building, Jona and Remi were immersed in paperwork related to the mating season protocols and procedures. Jona reiterated the importance of adhering to the mating guidelines set by the Ministry, and Remi readily agreed - in Crandon, strict adherence to regulations was paramount. Even the smallest deviation from the rules could disrupt the delicate balance of their precisely engineered society.

Inside the sterile research labs, scientists worked tirelessly conducting experiments to optimize fertility rates and genetic compatibility amongst Crandon's inhabitants. One scientist remarked to his colleague that they needed to ensure the genetic pool remained diverse - the very future of their city depended on it. In Crandon, reproduction was approached with clinical precision and scientific objectivity. Emotional factors like and attraction were considered secondary to the need for genetic compatibility and maximum productivity.

At the city's Education Center, young adults attended mandatory classes on reproductive health and genetic screening. The instructor drilled into them that their primary civic duty was to mate and produce offspring in order to ensure the continuation of Crandonian society. They were told to choose their mates wisely, based solely on scientific criteria rather than passion or romance.

That night in her compact apartment, Jona reviewed her own genetic profile, carefully analyzing the potential mates that had been selected for her by the government's complex matching algorithms. As the mating season approached, individuals awaited the revelation of their assigned reproductive partners, knowing their mating decisions would impact the collective future of Crandon.

At the government office, Jona and Remi attended a briefing on the final preparations leading up to the highly anticipated mating period. A Ministry official stressed that the success of the mating season was crucial for maintaining Crandon's societal stability into the next generation. He ordered staff to ensure all protocols were followed to the letter during this sensitive time.

When the long-awaited day finally arrived, the entire population of Crandon gathered together in the central city square for a ceremonial event marking the official commencement of mating season. As the city prepared to embark on another round of scientifically engineered reproduction, a heavy atmosphere settled amongst the inhabitants, all bracing themselves for the inevitable changes that lay ahead.

In the days leading up to the mating period, a nervous energy charged the air of Crandon with anticipation. The looming event cast an ever-growing shadow over the routines of the city. Beneath the veneer of order and control, anxieties brewed amongst the populace.

Alone in her apartment, Jona paced back and forth, consumed by conflicting emotions regarding the impending assigned mating that would shape the rest of her life according to Crandon's design.

Alone in her apartment, Jona spoke aloud to herself, questioning why she felt such unease rather than excitement about the impending assigned mating. She glanced anxiously at the government dossier containing clinical details about the stranger chosen to be her mate. For Jona and many others, the prospect of mating with someone selected purely on genetic metrics rather than actual attraction triggered uncertainty.

In his own living quarters, Remi sat troubled as he contemplated the regimented mating season fast approaching. He let out a heavy sigh, questioning aloud why it felt like they were all just cogs in some societal machine. Staring pensively out his window, Remi's mind swirled with conflicted thoughts. Like Jona, he struggled against the constraints of Crandon's rigid norms which suppressed basic human instincts and desires.

At the government building, Jona and Remi attended a mandatory pre-mating briefing, their faces etched with apprehension. A Ministry official reinforced that adherence to mating protocols was essential and that any deviations would not be tolerated. Jona and Remi exchanged uneasy glances, silently questioning the overwhelming control imposed upon them by the government.

THE MATING SEASON

Alone again that night in her apartment, Jona fought to suppress the primal urges welling up inside her, whispering to herself that she must resist these feelings that went against her societal conditioning. She struggled against her natural biological instincts, torn between obedience to Crandonian order and her own inner desires.

In his dim apartment, Remi sat in mental anguish, questioning if blindly following orders was all there was to life. He clenched his fists in frustration as the primal urges within him strained against his conditioned restraint.

As the mating season approached, both Jona and Remi found themselves at an inner crossroads, tempted by their instincts to rebel against the conformity demanded by their government. The city itself seemed to pulse with anticipation and uncertainty, on the brink of upheaval.

When the long-awaited mating season finally commenced, Crandon was plunged into tumultuous chaos. The carefully constructed facade of order disintegrated instantly in the face of uncontrollable biological urges.

On the first day, citizens roamed the streets with wild abandon, their once orderly behavior replaced entirely by primal reproductive instinct.

The need to mate took precedence above all else, with basic animal instincts now reigning supreme across the city.

Jona hesitated outside her apartment door, heart pounding with uncertainty. Though duty compelled her to mate with her government-assigned partner, she found herself drawn to the possibility of something deeper. The lines between obligation and desire blurred as primal urges consumed her.

In his own quarters, Remi struggled against the primal needs threatening to overwhelm his restraint. He longed to satisfy his instincts, yet also desired a meaningful connection beyond Crandon's clinical dictates. He was torn between reproductive duty and the hope for something more.

Amidst the frenzied chaos in the city square, Jona and Remi's paths fatefully crossed. Their eyes locked in a moment of undeniable connection, sparking a chemistry that defied their society's constraints.

Seeking refuge from the mayhem, they found themselves alone in an abandoned building. Breathing heavily, their hearts racing as they succumb to the pull of their emotions. Later, standing together on a rooftop gazing out at the disorder below, they found solace in each other's company despite the uncertainty ahead. A new bond had formed, transcending Crandon's regimented dictates.

As primal urges fueled the chaotic revolt, Crandon's leaders scrambled to restore order, desperately clinging to the belief that absolute governance and conformity were essential for stability.

In emergency meetings, government officials discussed strategies to quell the uprising, their expressions grave. The Minister insisted order must be restored by any means necessary before the rebellion spread further. But a dissenting Council Member cautioned that further suppressing the populace's free will could risk provoking greater unrest. The Minister remained firm - the city's stability was paramount, and total control must be maintained whatever the cost. Within the halls of power, dissent was swiftly stamped out as the authorities doubled down on their iron grip, determined to subdue the chaos at all costs.

In the city square, protesters gathered in defiance, chanting loudly for freedom and railing against the oppressive Ministry. They waved banners with slogans demanding autonomy and personal liberties, refusing to be silenced despite the government's crackdown on dissent.

Under cover of night, Jona and Remi met with fellow rebels in the abandoned building, their faces illuminated by flickering candlelight. The rebel leader addressed the group, declaring it was time to rise up and fight for their freedom against the Ministry's tyranny. Jona and Remi voiced their determination to take a stand, no matter the risks or consequences. The other rebels nodded solemnly in agreement; their resolve unwavering. In the shadows, a resistance movement was taking shape, fueled by the desire for self-determination.

On the streets, government agents maintained an intimidating presence, harshly reminding citizens of the penalties for disobedience. Fear and apprehension gripped the population as the authorities tightened their iron grip in response to the brewing unrest.

The struggle between draconian control and the stirrings of rebellion reached a boiling point as the city teetered on the brink of revolution. From City Hall, the Minister delivered a televised address, his voice echoing as he implored citizens to submit to the government's will for the sake of societal stability. But his words only steeled the rebels' defiance.

As Crandon hung precariously in the balance between order and chaos, the fate of its inhabitants rested on a knife's edge. They faced an impossible choice - take a stand for freedom despite the risks, or resign themselves to the comfort of conformity and control. The city pulsed with uncertainty as both sides readied themselves for the pivotal moment that would determine Crandon's future.

As mating frenzy consumed Crandon, Jona and Remi navigated the feverish crowds, their faces etched with determination and uncertainty. Swept up in the chaos, they were awash in a whirlwind of emotions.

Weaving through packed streets, they scanned the faces of potential mates with curiosity and apprehension. Jona shouted over the din, asking Remi if anyone stood out. Remi squinted and replied that everyone seemed interchangeable - despite the teeming hordes, they couldn't find a real connection.

Entering the bustling government mating center, designed to optimize matches scientifically, Jona grimaced. She despaired that they were expected to choose mates like data points on a graph, not complex human beings. Remi agreed it felt dehumanizing but saw no alternative within their regimented system. A feeling of disillusionment permeated the clinical space.

As the frenzied week neared its end, Jona and Remi felt increasing pressure to secure a mate before time ran out. The weight of permanent decisions bore down on them relentlessly.

Outside the mating center, anxiety crossed their faces as the final moment approached. Jona's voice trembled; unsure she could go through with permanently bonding to a stranger. Remi reassured her they had to choose and move forward - it was the only way. Steeling themselves, they entered to face the daunting task ahead.

Navigating crowded halls, their eyes darted between potential partners, desperately seeking a real connection. Jona agonized over making the wrong choice and regretting it forever. Remi squeezed her hand, promising they would figure it out together and to trust herself. Despite doubts, they persevered, determined to find the right match against the clock.

Sitting across from each other in a sterile matching room, Jona and Remi's hearts pounded. Jona whispered shakily that this was their last chance to choose their fate. Remi took a deep breath, vowing they could make the right decision together. Facing the biggest choice of their lives, they grappled with the enormity of the moment, knowing their options would forever shape their destiny.

Emerging from the matching room, relief and apprehension crossed Jona and Remi's faces. Jona exhaled deeply, stating it was done - they'd made their choices. Remi smiled weakly, hoping for the best. With matches secured, an uncertain future lay ahead.

Standing together in the city square as the mating week wound down, Jona's voice broke, realizing there was no going back. Remi squeezed her hand, vowing to face whatever came next together. As the sun set on Crandon, they stood united, ready to confront the challenges ahead.

With the mating frenzy over, Jona and Remi faced the aftermath of their pivotal decisions, knowing their lives were forever changed. A new chapter loomed, filled with uncertainty.

Alone in her apartment, Jona's thoughts swirled around the tumultuous week. She agonized over whether she'd made the right choice. Overwhelmed with doubt, the weight of her decision sat heavy.

Pacing his quarters, Remi's mind raced towards the future. He asked himself if they were truly ready for the responsibilities to come. Grappling with uncertainty, he struggled to accept the new reality.

Meeting in the square, anxiety crossed their faces as the next phase approached - pregnancy and parenthood. Jona worried they weren't ready or meant to be parents. Remi reassured her they'd figure it out together. Finding strength in each other, they braced for what lay ahead.

Sitting in the government building, anticipation pounded through them as they awaited pregnancy test results. Jona's voice shook, questioning their compatibility and abilities. But they drew solace from sharing these struggles. A solemn official entered, confirming they were deemed genetically compatible parents. Jona asked breathlessly what if they still failed, still weren't ready.

Facing impending parenthood with relative strangers, Jona and Remi wrestled with conforming to Crandon's rigid societal norms. After the frenzy of mating week, new challenges emerged - adjusting to unfamiliar partners and impending parental duties.

In her apartment, Jona sat with Lucas, her assigned partner. She forced a smile, saying she knew this wasn't expected but they had to make the best of it. Lucas nodded in agreement, claiming they'd figure it out. But an unease lingered between them.

With his partner Ella, Remi tentatively acknowledged this wasn't their choice, but they were in it together now. Ella forced a smile too, insisting they'd make it work. But as they navigated this arranged relationship, Remi and Ella struggled to find common ground amidst societal pressures.

Crossing paths in Crandon's bustling streets, Jona and Remi's eyes briefly met before continuing on. Jona softly asked how Remi was holding up; he forced a smile and said as well as could be expected. Jona admitted adjusting wasn't easy for her either.

Despite acting normal, an inner turmoil raged over their imposed lives.

In mandatory parenting classes, exhaustion shadowed Jona and Remi's faces as the instructor droned about raising good citizens. They felt resignation creep over them - in Crandon, conformity was enforced, not a choice. Jona despaired she wasn't cut out for this. Remi comfortingly reminded she wasn't alone.

As the mating cycle ended, Crandon resumed focus on other matters. But Jona and Remi grappled with lingering memories and emotions from the tumultuous week, its shadow hanging over them.

Alone in her apartment, lost in thought, Jona murmured to herself that it was over, yet nothing felt changed. The memories remained raw and unresolved; the emotions still present despite time moving on.

Standing at his window overlooking the city, Remi wondered if they'd ever truly be free from this society's constraints. As he grappled with doubts, he questioned if Crandon would allow its citizens to break the reproductive cycle.

Returning to work, Jona and Remi wore masks of determination, immersing themselves in tasks. Jona stated they must keep moving forward, not let the past define them. She insisted they'd find a way to break the cycle.

With biological roles complete, the inhabitants faced an existential crossroads. What came next in a society fixated on mating as life's primary purpose? Seeking meaning beyond the confines, they questioned their reason for being.

Alone in her mundane apartment, Jona stared pensively out the window. She murmured to herself, wondering if this was all there was to life. Contemplating her future, she felt there must be more than just fulfilling Crandon's expectations.

Pacing his quarters, Remi's mind fixated on finding purpose and meaning. He expressed frustration that life seemed an endless mating and reproduction cycle. Struggling for answers, his sense of disillusionment grew within the dictatorial society. Meeting on city streets, Jona and Remi mirrored each other's frustrations. Jona's voice filled with determination - they couldn't let this society dictate their purpose. There must be a way to break free of its constraints. Remi agreed, but how? They were just cogs in the machine. How to find meaning when valued only for reproduction? Together they took solace in their shared desire to seek out greater purpose beyond Crandon's shackles.

Side by side in the library, Jona and Remi poured over books, seeking answers. Jona excitedly proposed there could be a whole world beyond Crandon to explore and find their destinies. Remi's eyes lit up - anything was better than feeling trapped here. Researching, they felt drawn to life's possibilities outside Crandon.

In Crandon's heart, Jona and Remi were surrounded by questioning citizens. Jona proclaimed it was time to reclaim their freedom and right to choose their paths, after too long under burdensome expectations. Remi urged them not to let fear hold them back - change was possible by challenging the status quo. A spark of rebellion ignited in the restless crowd.

Before the Council, Jona and Remi's voices remained steady, demanding rights to choose their destinies without reproductive obligations or mandated pairings. Remi stated Crandon must celebrate individuality over conformity. The uneasy Council recognized the growing dissent.

Transformation swept Crandon as people openly questioned rigid norms, embracing newfound freedoms. Jona smiled that change was in the air. Remi grinned it was because of their courage to envision a better future. Walking Crandon's streets, pride washed over them for setting this new course of freedom.

Suddenly, a deafening alarm blared through the city. Jona and Remi exchanged shocked expressions. Around them, panic erupted. They realized their freedom fight was not over - something unexpected was about to upend everything.

Chaos erupted in the city square as citizens fled the alarming noise. Jona and Remi stood frozen in shock. Jona shouted over the din, demanding to know what was happening. Remi frantically looked around before pulling her to safety.

Bursting into a secret government building, the muffled alarm still droned. Breathless, Jona wondered if they'd launched a counterattack. Remi was unsure, but something felt very wrong. Moving cautiously onward, strange pulsing organic forms covered the walls. Jona nervously asked what this place was - she'd never seen anything like it. Remi urged her to keep moving, an ominous unease growing.

Entering a large chamber, mysterious organic pods lined the walls, seeming to react to their presence. Jona and Remi hesitated, filled with foreboding.

Jona whispered to Remi that she thought something was inside the pods. One began opening, a humanoid hand grasping the edge, making Jona SCREAM as Remi pulled her back protectively. A naked humanoid emerged, covered in fluid, rasping "Welcome..."

Horror flooded Jona and Remi as more pods opened, revealing dozens of cloned humanoids. Stunned, Remi realized this was Crandon's secret breeding lab they'd hidden. The humanoids shambled towards them menacingly as they clutched each other in terror. Jona shouted they had to escape immediately!

Running through twisting corridors, they desperately sought an exit while inhuman screams and shuffling footsteps pursued them relentlessly. Reaching a dead-end locked door, they pounded helplessly. The humanoids cornered them, grasping outstretched. Jona and Remi braced for the end.

Suddenly the wall crumbled beside them and a hand pulled them to safety into a secret tunnel just as the humanoids attacked. Their savior was Dax, a wild-eyed rebel, who urgently warned more were coming and they had to keep moving. Still shocked, Jona and Remi followed him deeper as distant alarms wailed. Their fight was just beginning.

Led through flickering tunnels, they arrived at a heavy metal door where Dax knocked in a coded pattern. It opened into a large chamber filled with rugged rebels who cheered at Dax's return. Their leader stepped forward, welcoming Jona and Remi, eager to help any enemy of Crandon. Jona asked what was happening and the meaning of the alarm. The leader declared it a call to action - Crandon's lies would pacify them no more.

Remi stated they wanted to help end Crandon's lifelong control over them. The rebels murmured approval. The leader said they'd need all the help they could get and showed them his attack plans.

In the tunnels, pairs of rebels navigated towards the surface, Jona and Remi among them. At a ladder, Dax whispered it was time to join the others above ground. Exchanging an apprehensive but resolved glance, they emerged into Crandon, now a battleground.

Sneaking through back alleys, they evaded laser fire to reach a shelter for rebel survivors. Helping the wounded, Jona and Remi saw war's grim reality, realizing the cost of their noble crusade. Shaken, Remi questioned if freedom was worth this. Resolute, Jona stated they couldn't turn back now, no matter the sacrifice.

Bloodied, Dax approached saying the rebel leader needed them urgently across the city. Jona and Remi steeled themselves and followed him out towards the chaotic streets once more.

A fierce battle raged in the city square as lasers crisscrossed through the darkness and rebels clashed with soldiers. Taking cover, Jona, Remi and Dax were joined by the rebel leader, face obscured. She declared they would attack on her signal, leading the rebels to swarm into the square.

Removing her helmet, the leader revealed herself to be Ella, Remi's former assigned mate. Her eyes blazed with ferocity as she stated Crandon would die so something better could rise from its ashes. Shocked, Jona could only stare as Ella gave the signal.

With heavy hearts, Jona and Remi raised their weapons, realizing Crandon's fate now rested in their hands alone. They followed Ella into the fray, though ghosts of the old Crandon already haunted them.

As dawn's first light peeked over smoke-wreathed ruins, the battle ended. Jona and Remi huddled in an alley, faces haggard, clothes torn. Jona numbly stated Crandon had fallen. Remi questioned if it was worth the terrible cost. Nearby, Dax defiantly dug through rubble and spat on a tattered Crandon flag, declaring them all free now.

But Jona felt no freedom, only uncertainty of who would lead and guide them next. Then Ella appeared, power and confidence emanating from her as she stated a new society would rise from Crandon's ashes, one where they controlled their own fates.

Uneasy, Remi asked hadn't enough died for her vision, when would it end? Ella coldly demanded they stand with her or face consequences. Her forces gathered behind her, ready to crush any remaining resistance.

Facing an impossible choice, Jona and Remi braced themselves for the continuing fight ahead. Crandon's ruins smoldered as they steeled themselves against Ella's iron will. The battle for freedom was won, but their future remained unwritten.

Standing before Ella in her stark new headquarters, Jona cautiously asked how they could trust her leadership after such bloodshed. Slamming her fist, Ella retorted she had freed them all - sacrifices were necessary. But Remi countered at what cost? So many lives lost...

With contempt, Ella asked who should lead instead. Jona placated her, saying they only wanted to ensure all voices were heard, unlike Crandon. Ella softened slightly with a sigh, agreeing an open council was prudent. Relieved, Jona and Remi pledged their support in gathering compassionate minds to rebuild together.

In the damaged city square, Jona and Remi passed Ella briefing workers. Jona hoped she'd be a just leader after all. But Dax emerged from shadows, warning Ella craved power and they shouldn't trust her words. Remi countered she'd agreed to share leadership. Dax scoffed words were meaningless until proven.

His skepticism lingered as Jona and Remi surveyed the ruins. Could Ella bring order or just more tyranny?

Inside the new council chamber, optimism mingled with tension as Jona and Remi met with Ella and three potential members, selected for their wisdom and empathy. One member expressed belief this council marked a hopeful new dawn for the people. Murmurs of agreement followed, while Ella scanned their faces, seeming to calculate their loyalty. She stated together they would create a just society, but difficult decisions lay ahead.

Ella outlined plans to overhaul industry and housing. Some ideas seemed reasonable; others bordered on autocratic. Exchanging subtle concerned glances, Jona and Remi questioned if she was already overreaching her authority.

In the city square, Ella announced her sweeping plans from atop a makeshift stage. While some cheered, others looked uneasy at her authoritarian tone. Watching anxiously from the crowd, Jona turned to Remi and urgently warned Ella's hunger for power was dangerous. Resolute, Remi agreed they must restrain her before she became a tyrant. Moving through the crowd, newly united in resolve, they sought to stop her.

Meeting the council members secretly, Jona and Remi discussed removing Ella from leadership. But without consensus, doing so risked greater turmoil. They strategized late into the night, hoping to balance principle and pragmatism.

Someone pounded frantically on Jona's door - it was a bloodied Dax; warning Ella had branded all dissenters enemies of the republic. He urged Jona to flee and inform the council that the fight for freedom wasn't over yet. As Dax disappeared into the night, Jona hurriedly packed a bag, now a fugitive in the city she'd helped liberate.

Jona met his gaze, understanding the reckless bravery that fueled his plea. "We cannot afford open confrontation yet," she countered gently. "But there's always a way to strike."

A spark lit in Remi's eyes. He'd spent weeks studying the communication channels used by Ella's forces. "Disinformation," he said. "We can sow discord in their ranks. Lead them away, create confusion..."

Jona saw the potential. "Yes! It's risky, but if we can create a large enough distraction..."

Their plan took shape - forged in desperate hope and a desire to protect those who couldn't fight back. Using captured equipment and Remi's technical prowess, they crafted false orders, rumors of rebel uprisings, and fabricated troop movements, feeding them into enemy channels.

The results were astounding. Ella's forces were scrambled, units sent chasing shadows while Jona's rebels staged daring raids on supply convoys, further adding to the chaos. The town, meanwhile, caught a fragile breath. Ella's troops, distracted and confused, were slow to respond to the unrest brewing there. This gave crucial time for many of the town's artists and healers to vanish into the hills, aided by a secret network of sympathizers.

News of the town's defiance spread like wildfire amongst the rebels. Jona, though relieved, kept her focus sharp. This was merely a skirmish won, not the war. Still, Ella had been rattled, and for the first time in months, there was a whisper of hope amongst the downtrodden.

Jona knew that their respite would be short-lived. Ella would double down on hunting them, her methods growing more ruthless. Yet, in this small victory, Jona saw the power of the human spirit – the stubborn will to fight, to subvert, even in the face of overwhelming odds. It was a flame she vowed to protect.

Winter tightened its grip, its icy fingers reaching into the rebel camp, testing the limits of their resilience. But the success of their recent operation had sparked a flicker of rebellion throughout the land. Whispers of defiance reached them from distant towns, relayed by a growing network of sympathizers. Jona felt the tide shifting, ever so slightly.

One crisp morning, a young scout stumbled into the camp, his face pale with fear. "They've found us," he gasped, "They're coming in force."

Jona's heart pounded. This was the moment they had dreaded, the inevitable confrontation. Despite their recent ingenuity, they were vastly outnumbered and under-equipped. Gathering the rebels, she addressed them with a voice that belied her own trepidation.

"We knew this day would come," she said, her gaze sweeping across the determined faces. "We have two options: fight, knowing we might fall, or surrender, allowing Ella to extinguish the flame of freedom."

A murmur rippled through the crowd. Jona saw the raw fear simmering beneath the surface, but also an unwavering defiance.

A young woman, barely eighteen, stepped forward, her voice ringing with conviction. "We fight, Jona. We fight for our loved ones, for the world we dream of. We fight for Ario's memory!"

A collective roar of agreement erupted, echoing through the snow-laden pines. Jona felt a surge of pride and a deep responsibility wash over her. These people, these rebels, were her family now, and their fight, her fight.

forces were a constant threat, but the rebels were becoming masters of evasion, disappearing into the landscape.

Finally, after weeks of careful travel, they arrived at a nondescript crossroads. A woman, plain and unassuming, stood there, a single candle flickering in her hand. She met Jona's eyes, then nodded toward a hidden trail winding into the hills.

The City of Passion was far more than a haven. It was a thriving community hidden in plain sight– nestled within forgotten valleys and abandoned settlements, connected by covert channels and networks of trust.

Here, Jona found the means to shift the fight. It wasn't about technology or weapons, but the power of ideas. The city became the unseen heart of the rebellion, fueling its spirit, and gradually undermining Ella's authority.

Finally, a year after her escape from Crandon, Jona returned. Ella's grip had weakened, and the hearts of the people were primed for change.

As Ella addressed the crowd, her voice laced with icy control, Jona felt a surge of defiance. She could remain hidden, a silent observer, but that wouldn't change the future she envisioned.

With a deep breath, she stepped forward, her heart pounding against her ribs. The guards immediately seized her, their faces contorted with suspicion. Ella, her eyes narrowed, turned towards Jona, a flicker of curiosity battling the usual imperiousness in her gaze.

Jona lifted her chin, her voice carrying the weight of countless suppressed voices. "I still a citizen of Crandon, a city robbed of its soul," she proclaimed. "I come not with weapons, but with a plea for understanding."

Ella scoffed, a harsh sound that sent shivers down the spines of those gathered. "Understanding? This rebellion has brought only chaos and disruption."

Jona countered, holding out the locket.

Your control may bring order, but it extinguishes the very essence of humanity."

She opened the locket, its worn corners cradling a past Ella had tried to erase. A woman, with eyes that mirrored Jona's defiant spirit, smiled from the picture, holding hands with another woman, their love a defiance of Ella's forced conformity.

A flicker of surprise crossed Ella's face, a momentary glimpse of the woman she might have been, the woman whose ideals had been twisted by the burden of power. Jona saw it, a vulnerability hidden beneath layers of icy control.

Taking a step closer, Jona lowered her voice, a tremor of vulnerability underlying her steely resolve. "There is another way, Ella. A way where everyone can choose their path, where love and desires are not dictated by an external force."

As Jona spoke, a strange hush fell over the crowd. Even the guards seemed to hold their breath, captivated by the unexpected exchange.

Ella stared at Jona; her face unreadable. The coldness in her eyes seemed to falter, replaced by an emotion Jona couldn't decipher. Then, in a gesture as unexpected as the entire encounter, Ella closed the gap between them.

Their lips met, a brief touch that resonated like a thunderclap in the silence. Jona had expected resistance, anger, even violence. But none of that came. Instead, she felt a tremor, a flicker of something akin to pain in Ella's touch, a yearning for something lost.

When Ella pulled back, her eyes were glistening with unshed tears. The harsh lines of her face seemed to soften, replaced by a profound sadness. Jona saw not an enemy, but a woman burdened by the weight of a power built on fear and control.

"I see," Ella whispered, her voice barely audible. "I see what I have lost." The weight of those words hung heavy in the air. With a shaky hand, Ella lowered her weapon, the sound echoing through the stunned crowd. She turned to her guards; her voice hoarse but firm.

"Stand down," she commanded. "We return to headquarters."

The guards, their faces mirroring the stunned confusion of the crowd, obeyed. As Ella turned to leave, she paused and looked at Jona, a flicker of gratitude battling the remnants of her imperious facade. Then, without another word, she disappeared into the night, her silhouette fading into the darkness.

News of Ella's visit and her encounter with Jona spread like wildfire. The city erupted in cautious celebration. Whispers of rebellion morphed into open murmurs of hope. Jona became a symbol, her courage and compassion igniting a spark in the hearts of the oppressed.

However, the victory was fragile. Ella's withdrawal wasn't a complete surrender, but a tactical retreat. She remained at the helm, her loyal guard still in control, her forces still patrolling the streets. The question hung heavy in the air: what did Ella's actions signify?

Days turned into weeks, then months. While no major battles erupted, Crandon became a battleground of subtle defiance.

One scorching afternoon, a young boy named Loui, barely ten years old, approached the central market, clutching a single sunflower. The market, once bustling with life, had become a shell of its former self, fear casting a long shadow over the once vibrant stalls.

As Loui walked through the aisles, offering his sunflower to anyone who would dare accept it, whispers started. People, hesitant at first, began to smile, their eyes glimmering with a forgotten joy. Some even dared to buy small trinkets from the vendors, a silent act of defiance against the enforced austerity.

The guards, ever watchful, spotted Loui. They approached him, their faces grim. "What are you doing here, boy?" the gruff leader barked.

Loui, his voice trembling slightly, held up thesunflower. "It's beautiful, isn't it? Just like freedom."

The guard's eyes flickered. He looked at the faces of the surrounding crowd, the subtle gestures of defiance now impossible to ignore. His hand hovered over his blaster, uncertainty clouding his features. Then, in a moment that defied expectations, he lowered his weapon.

"Just get out of here, kid," he mumbled, turning away.

This small act, witnessed by many, became another turning point. It showed the fragility of Ella's control, the cracks in the foundation of her regime. The fear still lingered, but so did hope, nurtured by the seeds of courage and compassion Jona had sown.

Meanwhile, within the sterile confines of the government headquarters, Ella grappled with turmoil. Jona's words echoed in her mind, a constant reminder of the life she once envisioned, a life dedicated to equality and freedom. The power she now wielded felt heavy, a burden that choked the spirit she once possessed.

She looked at her reflection in the chrome surface of her desk. The woman staring back had the same sharp features, the same piercing eyes, but they held a newfound vulnerability. The encounter with Jona had shattered the mask of cold authority she had worn for so long, forcing her to confront the truth about her own desires.

One evening, Ella found herself drawn to the archives, a dusty repository of Crandon's forgotten history. Here, amidst old photographs and faded documents, she stumbled upon a record of her younger self, a passionate young woman who had fought for the very freedoms she now suppressed.

As she poured over the documents, tears welled up in her eyes. She saw a reflection of the woman Jona had shown her, the woman she could have been, the woman she longed to be again.

Fuelled by this newfound clarity, Ella made a decision. She summoned her advisors, the men who had bolstered her rise to power, the architects of the regime she now despised. As they entered her office, their faces etched with anticipation, they were met with a different Ella, a woman who spoke with newfound conviction.

"We are changing course," she declared, her voice firm, her eyes burning with a fire long extinguished. "The suppression of free will will end. We will build a society based on choice, where individual expression and diversity are celebrated, not condemned."

Her advisors were stunned. Some protested, clinging to the old order. Others, sensing the inevitable shift, cautiously pledged their support. Ella, however, knew the road ahead wouldn't be easy. Rebuilding trust, dismantling the machinery of control, and fostering a culture of free will would be a monumental task.

But she was determined. Inspired by Jona's unwavering faith in humanity, she embarked on a journey of reconciliation. She met with leaders of the rebellion, not as adversaries, but as fellow citizens seeking a brighter future.

Jona, initially cautious, approached with an open mind. Her rebel times had honed her skills as a negotiator, and she saw the glimmer of genuine change in Ella's eyes.

Together, they embarked on a series of workshops and discussions, Jona stepped into the once-oppressive halls of government headquarters, apprehension tinged with a glimmer of hope. This building, once a symbol of ironclad control, now hummed with the energy of change.

She was greeted by Ella, no longer the imposing figure from their past encounters, but a woman etched with the lines of introspection and burdened with the weight of a new responsibility: rebuilding trust after years of suppression.

"Jona," Ella said, her voice quieter than Jona remembered, "thank you for coming."

Jona nodded, acknowledging the unspoken gratitude. Together, they entered the conference room, a space pulsating with nervous anticipation. Representatives from various factions across Crandon, once divided by ideology and fear, now shared the round table.

Jona scanned the room. There were faces hardened by years of struggle, eyes haunted by memories of oppression, and others filled with a tentative hope. This was a delicate dance, a negotiation not just of political agendas, but of emotions and deeply rooted biases.

Jona took the lead, her voice infused with the wisdom she had gathered in the City of Passion. "We gather here not as victors or vanquished," she began, "but as fellow citizens of Crandon, united by a shared desire for a better future."

She acknowledged the pain inflicted by Ella's regime, the suppression of free expression, the stifling of individual aspirations. But she also spoke with empathy, acknowledging the fear and uncertainty that had driven Ella's actions.

"Fear can be a powerful motivator," Jona said, "but it can also build walls, separating us from understanding and compassion."

Her words resonated with many. A young artist, Maria, whose vibrant murals had become symbols of defiance, spoke next.

"We cannot erase the past," she said, her voice trembling slightly, "but we can choose how we move forward. Can we forgive, not to condone the past, but to break free from its shackles?"

Others shared their experiences, voicing fears and anxieties, but also offering ideas for reconstruction. A scientist, ostracized for his independent research under the old regime, spoke of the need for open communication and the freedom of pursuing knowledge.

The discussions continued for days, fueled by raw emotions and a fragile hope. There were clashes, disagreements, and moments of strained silence. Yet, Jona held firm to the principles of open dialogue and mutual respect, guiding the group towards common ground.

Ella, throughout the process, remained an active participant. She acknowledged her mistakes, taking responsibility for the pain inflicted upon Crandon. She listened attentively to the voices of her citizens, their concerns and aspirations shaping her own perspective.

Slowly, the ice around her heart began to melt, replaced by a sense of responsibility and a yearning to atone for her past. She proposed dismantling the surveillance equipment, releasing political prisoners, and establishing an independent judiciary.

These initial steps, although seemingly small, were met with cautious optimism. The dismantling of surveillance towers became a powerful symbol of the regime's retreat, while the release of prisoners triggered emotional reunions and a wave of relief across the city.

However, the task of rebuilding trust was far from complete. Scars from the past ran deep, and anxieties lingered. Whispers of doubt and mistrust still echoed in some corners, a reminder of the challenges ahead.

One evening, as disagreements flared during a particularly difficult discussion, Jona stepped outside the conference room, seeking a moment of respite. She found Ella standing on the balcony, gazing at the city bathed in the orange hues of the setting sun.

"This is harder than I imagined," Ella admitted, her voice laced with exhaustion. "The damage runs deeper than I realized."

Jona placed a hand on her shoulder, a gesture of silent encouragement. "Rebuilding trust takes time," she said, "but remember, every step forward, no matter how small, is a step toward a better future."

Ella looked at Jona, her eyes searching. "Do you truly believe we can overcome this? Can this city become the haven you envisioned, a place where freedom and diversity are truly valued?"

Jona met her gaze, her own filled with unwavering conviction. "I do," she said. "But it will require all of us. It will require the courage to forgive, the willingness to listen, and the commitment to create a future where the power of free will shines brighter than any fear."

Chapter III

Aeons

THE CITY HUMMED WITH the energy of reconstruction. Jona, her hands calloused from countless meetings and discussions, felt a familiar sense of purpose. Yet, amidst the celebrations and rebuilding efforts, a gnawing unease lingered within her. It was a memory, a fragment from the turbulent days of the rebellion, a memory of fleeting encounters with the strange, humanoid figures who had appeared and vanished just as quickly, leaving her with more questions than answers.

These encounters, though brief, had been deeply unsettling. The humanoids, possessed an otherworldly grace and an unnerving silence.

They had seemed to observe the rebellion from the shadows, their motives and origins shrouded in mystery. Jona, consumed by the immediate struggles of the revolution, had pushed these encounters to the back of her mind.

However, as she sifted through the chaos of her memories, a single, unsettling detail resurfaced. The humanoids clones had possessed the same mark – a swirling symbol etched onto their palms; a symbol that bore a striking resemblance to the ancient glyphs Jona had encountered in the City of Passion.

The glyphs, according to the wisdom shared by the city's elders, were whispers of a forgotten past, hinting at a time when humanity coexisted with beings of an otherworldly nature. These beings, the elders explained, possessed advanced technology and knowledge, knowledge that both fascinated and frightened the habitants of that era.

Driven by this newfound urgency, Jona sought out Remi, her trusted companion. He, too, had witnessed them on the periphery of the rebellion, their otherworldly presence leaving him equally perplexed.

"The symbol," Jona said, tracing the swirling pattern in the air. "It's the same symbol from the City of Passion, the one associated with those... beings from the legends."

Remi, his brow furrowed in thought, nodded. "Intriguing. Could there be a connection? Did Ella know something about them?"

"It's possible," Jona mused. "The resources at her disposal, the technology... perhaps she had some knowledge, some way of communicating with them."

Fueled by their curiosity, Jona and Remi embarked on a clandestine investigation. They delved into Ella's confiscated archives, sifting through cryptic files and research reports. Days turned into weeks, and their search yielded a single, tantalizing clue – a fragmented message, intercepted by Ella's forces years ago, addressed to "the Protector" in a language far beyond their comprehension.

The message, though incomplete, sent shivers down their spines. It spoke of an impending event, a "convergence," and hinted at a hidden sanctuary within the city, a place unknown even to Ella's regime. Armed with this newfound information, Jona and Remi decided to reach out to the elders of the City of Passion. Perhaps, within their ancient knowledge, they might find answers to the mysteries surrounding the strange figures and the enigmatic message.

The journey back to the city was fraught with challenges. Ella's influence still lingered in certain pockets, and remnants of her security forces patrolled the outskirts. Yet, fueled by their growing sense of urgency, they navigated the hidden routes and reached the city undetected.

The elders, wise and ageless, listened intently to Jona's account. Recognition flickered in their eyes as she spoke of the symbol and the intercepted message.

"The beings you encountered," the eldest began, his voice raspy with age, "are known as the Aeons. The revelation from the elders hit Jona like a physical blow. The elusive figures, the unsettling observations, the cryptic message – they all pointed to a horrifying truth.

The Aeons weren't mere observers; they were orchestrators, manipulating the lives of Crandon's citizens for their own purposes.

"Mating season?" Remi echoed, his voice tight with disgust. "They don't see us as equals, do they? We're just... cattle to them."

Jona fought back a wave of nausea. The weight of this knowledge pressed down on her, shattering the fragile hope she had nurtured. Years of struggle, of fighting for freedom, only to discover they were never truly free.

The elders, sensing their despair, offered a flicker of solace. "While the Aeons' methods are indeed manipulative, they are not inherently malevolent. Their goal, as they perceive it, is to ensure the survival and evolution through careful selection."

"By controlling our lives, our choices?" Jona spat. "That's not evolution, it's enslavement."

"It is a complex situation," the elder replied calmly. "But remember, they are not omnipotent. They might track our choices, but they cannot control them entirely.

The power of free will, however suppressed, still exists."

These words sparked a flicker of rebellion within Jona. If the Aeons relied on data to make their selections, then perhaps they could disrupt the system. They could introduce chaos into the data, making it impossible for the Aeons to make accurate predictions.

"We can fight back," Remi stated, a glint of determination in his eyes. "We can flood their system with false data, confuse their algorithms. Jona, you know this city better than anyone. We can use its hidden passageways, its forgotten corners, to create a blind spot, a sanctuary from their monitoring."

Jona felt a surge of renewed determination. This wasn't about creating a perfect society; it was about safeguarding the most fundamental right – the right to choose one's own path. She shared Remi's plan with the elders, and after careful consideration, they offered their support.

They revealed the existence of forgotten networks, ancient tunnels burrowed deep beneath the city, built by the long-forgotten Protectors. These tunnels, invisible to the Aeons' technology, could be their haven, their base of operations.

Equipped with detailed maps and survival supplies, Jona and Remi embarked on their new mission. They led a small group of volunteers, individuals who had also witnessed the strange figures and were determined to fight for their autonomy.

The descent into the tunnels was like entering a forgotten world. The air, thick with the scent of damp earth and forgotten history, held a sense of both dread and possibility. As they navigated the labyrinthine network, Jona shared stories she had heard from the elders, tales of the Protectors' rebellion, their attempts to break free from the Aeons' influence.

Their journey was far from easy. The tunnels were filled with crumbling pathways, collapsed sections, and the constant threat of being discovered. But their resolve remained unwavering, fueled by the desire to reclaim their agency, their right to choose their partners, their futures.

Finally, they reached a hidden chamber, a vast cavern untouched by time. Here, they established their base, using the cavern's natural resources and Remi's expertise to create a communication network, a way to spread awareness and disrupt the Aeons' data collection.

Jona, with her deep understanding of Crandon's hidden corners, led team out of the tunnels, orchestrating acts of defiance. They staged fake encounters, created false narratives, and flooded the city with misinformation, creating a digital smokescreen that obscured their true intentions.

As weeks turned into months, the impact of their actions began to show. The Aeons' data became increasingly unreliable, their predictions thrown into disarray. The carefully curated mating season was thrown into chaos as planned pairings fell through, with individuals choosing to follow their own desires, defying the Aeons' preordained destiny.

This defiance, however, came at a cost. The Aeons, sensing the disruption in their system, grew irritated. Their presence in the city became more pronounced, their silent observations morphing into active interventions. Strange energy disruptions started occurring, communication channels went haywire, and an unsettling paranoia gripped the city.

Jona knew this was just the beginning. The Aeons, accustomed to controlling the narrative, wouldn't tolerate this rebellion for long. They would fight back, and the battle for Crandon's future was far from over.

As news of the new rebellion spread, fear and hope intertwined in Crandon's heart. While the hidden community thrived beneath the city, fear took hold of the surface world. The Aeons, their plans disrupted, began to flex their power. Eerie lights danced across the night sky, strange disruptions crippled communication networks, and whispers of disappearances fueled paranoia.

Jona, knew the fight was escalating. They needed allies, a way to bridge the gap between the hidden resistance and the people above. The elders, sensing her dilemma, proposed a daring plan - to reach out to Ella, offering partnership in this unexpected crisis.

The idea was met with skepticism. Ella, despite her efforts towards reform, was still mistrusted by many. But Jona saw a desperate gamble in this proposal. Ella, with her knowledge of the Aeons' technology, could be a valuable asset.

A risky infiltration operation was planned. Remi, disguised as an Aeon sympathizer, managed to reach Ella, conveying Jona's message. Ella, initially hesitant, was swayed by the evidence Remi presented – the disrupted data, the testimonies of those who had witnessed the Aeons' manipulation.

A secret meeting was arranged in the heart of the tunnels, cloaked in darkness and shrouded in uncertainty. Jona, tense but resolute, faced Ella, their past a stark contrast to the present.

"Ella," Jona began, her voice echoing in the cavern, "we are facing a threat that surpasses our past differences. The Aeons are not benevolent observers, but manipulators who control our lives for their own ends."

Ella listened intently, her face betraying a mix of disbelief and dawning comprehension. When Jona finished, a long silence filled the cavern. Then, with a sigh heavy with years of burden, Ella spoke.

"I see now the truth of my own blindness," she admitted. "I sought control, but I failed to see the larger truth, the one you reveal."

A fragile alliance was formed, an unlikely partnership built on the foundation of opposing the Aeons' dominion. Ella, with her access to some of the remaining government resources, helped decipher the Aeons' technology, uncovering their vulnerabilities.

Remi, his genius fueled by Ella's insights, created a device capable of creating localized disruptions in the Aeons' energy field. This device, however, was a double-edged sword. It could disrupt their monitoring, but it could also attract their attention, drawing them directly to the hidden base.

The decision to use it was fraught with risk. But with the Aeons' presence growing bolder, a gamble had to be taken. Jona, leading a team of volunteers, ventured out into the city, carrying the device concealed within an innocuous package.

They reached the heart of Crandon, a bustling plaza where the Aeons often surface for observation. As a crowd gathered, Jona activated the device. A ripple of distortion spread through the air, temporarily disrupting the Aeons' energy field.

For a moment, the figures flickered, their humanoid disguise forms wavering. Then, with a sound like a thunderclap, the device overloaded, its components spouting sparks. Jona and her team, their faces grim, threw themselves to the ground as the plaza erupted in blinding light.

When the light subsided, the plaza was empty. The Aeons had vanished, leaving behind a crater and a lingering sense of foreboding. Back in the hidden base, analyzing the data recovered from the device, Remi discovered a startling revelation. The Aeons, frustrated by the disrupted data, were planning a convergence event, a large-scale gathering that would amplify their energy field and grant them a more potent control over Crandon.

The elders, their faces etched with worry, explained the implications of this event. The convergence could potentially wipe out free will entirely, rendering Crandon's population mere puppets in the Aeons' control.

The situation was dire. Time was running out. Jona and her team realized they had to strike back, and this time, it had to be decisive. They had to prevent the convergence at all costs.

Using the knowledge gleaned from Ella and the fragmented data collected, they devised a plan. Their strategy was audacious, bordering on reckless. They would infiltrate the Aeons' hidden sanctuary, located somewhere within the city, and disrupt the convergence from its source.

The mission was fraught with danger. The Aeons' sanctuary, was nearly impenetrable. But Jona, fueled by a desperate hope and a newfound sense of unity shared with Ella and the others, led the team on their most perilous mission yet.

Jona gripped the device, its cold metal a stark contrast to the urgency burning in her heart. It pulsed faintly, suddenly Jona's breath caught in her throat. It was Ella, but not the Ella they knew. The once-stern leader was shrouded in glow, her features obscured. A flicker of surprise crossed Jona's face, then it settled into understanding. Ella, with a gesture of apology, revealing tear-streaked eyes filled with a mixture of shame and determination.

"Forgive me, Jona," she whispered, her voice raspy with unshed tears. "I was one of them, chosen by the Aeons to manipulate Crandon. But I saw the truth, the pain and suffering they inflicted. My will couldn't remain shackled any longer."

Jona and Remi exchanged nervous glances; their trust momentarily shaken. However, Ella's anguish seemed genuine, her plea laced with desperation.

"I know," Ella continued, her voice trembling, "you may not trust me, but I offer you something invaluable – knowledge about their weaknesses, their sanctuaries, their plans for the convergence."

Jona's mind raced. This unexpected revelation could be a game-changer, offering invaluable insight into the enemy's camp. With a deep breath, she decided to take a chance.

"Tell us everything," Jona said, her voice firm but laced with caution. "Tell us how to stop them."

Ella, visibly relieved, poured out her story. She spoke of her initial selection by the Aeons, her training in their manipulative techniques, and the growing disillusionment she experienced as she witnessed the suffering they inflicted.

She then revealed the location of their hidden sanctuary, a place of convergence where the Aeons would amplify their energy field, subduing the free will of Crandon's entire population.

"They believe themselves benevolent," Ella said, her voice filled with disgust, "but their forced control is no different from enslavement."

As Ella spoke, a plan, daring and precarious, began to take shape. Jona, Remi, and Ella would use her knowledge to infiltrate the Aeon sanctuary, aiming to disrupt the convergence from within. It was a suicide mission, fraught with danger and uncertainty.

However, the stakes were too high. Letting the convergence occur was unthinkable. They had to act, even if it meant risking everything.

With a shared sense of desperation and a flicker of newfound trust, they embarked on a clandestine mission unlike any other.

The tension was palpable, the weight of their mission a heavy burden on their shoulders.

Finally, they reached the Aeon sanctuary, a vast, cavernous space pulsating with an otherworldly energy. The air crackled with a strange hum, and in the center of the cavern, a swirling vortex of energy shimmered, the gateway to the convergence.

Jona's heart pounded in her chest as she witnessed the source of their oppression, the very technology that threatened to erase their free will. Remi, his hand resting on a hidden device designed to disrupt the energy flow, prepared for the most crucial act of their mission.

But before they could act, a booming voice echoed through the cavern, sending shivers down their spines. "Welcome, initiates. The time for convergence is upon us."

Jona's blood ran cold. They had been discovered. Standing before them was an Aeon, its eyes glowing with an unnerving intensity.

The Aeon, oblivious to their true identities, ushered them towards the convergence point. As they drew closer, Jona felt a strange pressure building up within her, a force attempting to manipulate her thoughts, to bend her will.

With a surge of defiance, she fought back, channeling the spirit of the rebellion, the years of struggle against oppression. She refused to succumb, her free will burning brighter than the Aeon's energy field.

Inspired by Jona's resistance, Ella and Remi joined the fight. Ella, her voice tinged with newfound strength, exposed their true identities and their mission to disrupt the convergence.

The Aeon, stunned by this revelation, retaliated with a blast of energy, forcing them to evade. A fierce battle ensued, a physical manifestation of their ongoing struggle for freedom against an entity that sought to control them.

Jona, Ella, and Remi, caught in the cavern's echoing battle, felt the force of the Aeon's energy blast singe their cloaks. They scattered, utilizing the cavern's vastness to evade further attacks.

Ella, her eyes blazing with a newfound fierceness, landed near the swirling vortex of the convergence point. She knew this was their only chance. With a battle cry that echoed through the cavern, she lunged towards the Aeon, unleashing every ounce of her pent-up anger and frustration.

The Aeon, caught off guard by this unexpected display of defiance, stumbled back. In that moment, Ella saw her opportunity. With a desperate surge of strength, she grappled the Aeon, throwing them both towards the convergence point. A blinding light erupted as they collided with the swirling energy vortex. The cavern trembled, and a deafening roar filled the air. The light intensified, engulfing the Aeon and Ella in its blinding embrace.

Jona and Remi, shielded by a rocky outcrop, watched in horror and awe as the light grew in intensity. The cavern walls groaned, threatening to crumble under the immense pressure.

Then, as abruptly as it began, the light subsided. Silence descended upon the cavern, broken only by the faint hum of the deactivated convergence point.

Jona and Remi cautiously emerged from their hiding place, their hearts pounding in their chests. The once vibrant sanctuary lay eerily still. The Aeons, their shimmering forms usually pulsing with energy, were now scattered around the cavern, unmoving, lifeless.

Ella lay amidst them, her body still, her features peaceful. A single tear traced its way down her cheek, a testament to the sacrifice she had made.

Jona rushed to her side, her eyes filled with tears and a deep sense of gratitude. Ella, the once-manipulator, had become their unlikely savior, her final act a testament to the power of free will.

Remi surveyed the scene, his face etched with a mixture of relief and sorrow. The threat had been neutralized, but at a terrible cost. Ella's sacrifice would forever be etched in their memory, a reminder of the fight for freedom and the fragility of life.

News of the Aeons' demise spread like wildfire through Crandon. The city erupted in a mixture of joy and disbelief. The oppressive regime, the strange figures, the fear of manipulated destinies – all of it seemed like a distant nightmare.

Jona, addressing the city from a central plaza, her voice thick with emotion, spoke of Ella's sacrifice and the hard-fought victory. She urged Crandon not to mourn the past, but to learn from it, to cherish their newfound freedom, and to build a future where individuality and choice were not just privileges, but the very foundation of their society.

With the threat of the Aeons eradicated, Crandon embarked on a journey of rebuilding, not just infrastructure, but trust and unity. The hidden community, their purpose fulfilled, emerged from the shadows, integrating into the city.

The victory over the Aeons cast a long shadow over Crandon. The celebration of freedom was tinged with a profound sense of loss and a gnawing mistrust. While liberated from the Aeons' control, the city found itself grappling with a new and unforeseen dilemma – the infiltration of the Aeons themselves.

News of Ella's true identity, and the revelation that a significant portion of the population were unwittingly Aeon sympathizers, sent shockwaves through society. The lines between victim and perpetrator blurred, leaving behind a deep well of suspicion and fear.

Jona, burdened by the weight of this revelation, addressed the city once again, her voice heavy with sorrow. "We have to remember," she declared, "not all who were manipulated by the

Aeons were inherently evil. Many, like Ella, were forced, coerced, or deceived into serving their agenda."

Her words resonated with some, but many remained unconvinced. Families lay shattered, friendships broken, the very fabric of society strained under the weight of mistrust. Accusations flew, fingers pointed, and the city simmered on the edge of a volatile social unrest.

Remi, ever the pragmatist, proposed a solution – a truth commission. This commission, he suggested, would provide a platform for individuals to come forward and share their experiences, both victims and perpetrators alike. It would be a space for healing, forgiveness, and the arduous journey towards rebuilding trust.

The proposal was met with resistance. Some saw it as a betrayal of the fallen, a soft stance on those who had aided the Aeons. Others, however, recognized the need for reconciliation and understanding.

Ultimately, the commission was established, a fragile beacon of hope in a sea of uncertainty. Individuals came forward, sharing their stories – tales of manipulation, guilt, and the yearning for redemption. Some confessed to their actions, seeking forgiveness. Others, victims of the Aeons' deception, shared their pain and confusion.

The process was slow, riddled with emotional outbursts and painful confrontations. But slowly, amidst the tears and anger, a flicker of empathy began to emerge. People began to see each other not just as labels – Aeon sympathizer, victim, or hero – but as individuals, each with their own story, their own motivations, their own capacity for good and bad.

THE MATING SEASON

The journey towards rebuilding trust was arduous, filled with setbacks and moments of despair. However, with each honest conversation, each act of forgiveness, the cracks in Crandon's social fabric began to mend.

Amidst this process, a new political landscape emerged. Factions advocating for complete transparency and complete societal reform rose to prominence. Others championed a more cautious approach, emphasizing healing and reconciliation alongside necessary reforms.

The debate was fierce, at times bordering on the acrimonious. But through it all, the people of Crandon engaged in a vibrant political discourse, exercising the very freedom they had fought so hard to obtain.

The truth commission completed its work, leaving behind a legacy of collective healing and a blueprint for moving forward. The scars of the Aeon invasion remained, a constant reminder of the city's fragile freedom.

Crandon, forever changed by its encounter with the Aeons, continued to evolve. It became a society that valued free will while remaining cautious of external influences.

The first "Free Will Season" in Crandon's history dawned, carrying an air of anticipation and trepidation. The city, liberated from the Aeons and their manipulative matchmaking system, stood on the precipice of unprecedented choice. Gone were the pre-assigned partners, the orchestrated schedules, and the societal pressure to comply.

In their place lay a vast, uncharted territory – the freedom to choose one's own path, including the path of love and partnership.

However, this newfound freedom was a double-edged sword. Decades of government-controlled mating had instilled a sense of passivity and dependence within the population. While the desire for companionship burned bright, the act of initiating connection, of navigating the complexities of human interaction, felt like a foreign language.

In the bustling market square, typically a hub of vibrant human interaction, a curious stillness hung in the air. Young men and women, adorned in their finest attire, stole awkward glances at one another, their yearning masked by layers of uncertainty. Conversations, usually lively and effortless, faltered under the weight of potential rejection.

Jona, observing the scene from a distance, felt a pang of empathy. She understood their hesitance. Stepping outside the comfort zone of preordained pairings was a daunting task, especially for a generation conditioned to follow societal dictates.

She spotted Remi, his usual confident demeanor seemingly dampened by the atmosphere. "Looks like we're witnessing the birth pangs of real courtship," she quipped, her voice laced with a hint of amusement.

Remi chuckled, a hint of self-deprecation tinging his laughter. "Seems even the most tech-savvy can get tongue-tied when it comes to the matters of the heart."

They wandered through the market square, observing interactions, both successful and painfully awkward. A young man, gathering his courage, approached a woman only to trip over his words, his blushing face betraying his embarrassment. A group of women, emboldened by a shared frustration, decided to take control, engaging in lively discussions and forming unexpected connections.

As the days turned into weeks, a subtle shift began to take place. The initial awkwardness started to melt away, replaced by genuine attempts at connection.

Cafes became havens for budding conversations, parks echoed with laughter, and evenings were filled with impromptu gatherings, fueled by music and shared stories.

Jona and Remi, amidst their roles as community leaders, found themselves playing unexpected roles – matchmaking facilitators. They organized social events, encouraged ice-breaker activities, and offered guidance to those seeking advice on navigating the murky waters of romance.

The journey was far from smooth. Misunderstandings arose, hearts were broken, and rejection stung. Yet, with each stumble and fall, Crandon learned to navigate the unfamiliar terrain of free will. They discovered the joy of vulnerability, the thrill of genuine connection, and the profound significance of choosing one's own partner, not out of obligation, but out of love, respect, and shared desires.

Couples, hand-in-hand, strolled through the streets, their eyes sparkling with shared love and laughter. The market square, once a space of awkward encounters, now hummed with the energy of vibrant discussions, blossoming relationships, and the joy of discovering one another freely.

Jona, watching the scene from her balcony once again, felt a surge of pride. The seeds of courage, sown in the aftermath of the revolution, had blossomed into a beautiful, albeit imperfect, reality. Crandon, scarred but resilient, had taken its first steps towards a future where love was not dictated, but chosen, nurtured, and celebrated – a testament to the enduring power of free will and the human capacity for connection.

The first blush of "Free Will Season" in Crandon had faded, leaving behind an unexpected reality far harsher than anticipated. While the initial awkwardness had dissolved, replaced by a burgeoning vibrancy of connection, a new set of challenges began to emerge, threatening to engulf the city in a different kind of chaos.

The generations raised under the Aeons' control had been deprived of crucial social and emotional development. While the concept of free-will partnerships held immense romanticism, the reality of nurturing intimacy and navigating the complexities of emotional fulfillment proved far more complex than anticipated.

The city, once accustomed to the sterile efficiency of preordained compatibility, struggled to cope with the messy realities of human connection. Misunderstandings festered, fueled by a lack of communication skills and an inability to express emotions effectively. Communication, a skill previously unnecessary under programmed pairings, became a minefield, filled with misinterpretations and hurtful exchanges.

The consequences were swift and far-reaching. Broken relationships littered the city like fallen leaves. Unresolved conflicts escalated into bitter public spats, leaving emotional scars deeper than anyone anticipated. The joy of freedom morphed into a sense of overwhelming burden, the weight of choice pressing heavily on individuals ill-equipped to handle it.

Jona, witnessing the burgeoning crisis unfold, felt a sense of despair mingle with the remnants of hope. The fight against the Aeons had been arduous, but this new battle felt equally daunting, one fought not against external forces, but against the internal demons unleashed by newfound freedom.

She sought Remi, his usual optimistic demeanor clouded by worry. "We underestimated the impact of the Aeons' control," he admitted, his voice laced with frustration. "They may have been gone, but the emotional illiteracy they imposed lingers, threatening to unravel the very fabric of our society."

Together, they tackled the problem head-on. They established community forums, where individuals could share their experiences, learn healthy communication skills, and receive guidance from trained counselors. Workshops on emotional intelligence, conflict resolution, and navigating healthy relationships were organized, attracting large crowds eager to understand the complexities of navigating their newfound freedom.

The city council, recognizing the gravity of the situation, allocated resources to establish a comprehensive social support system. This included establishing childcare facilities, fostering responsible parenthood programs, and providing financial aid to single parents struggling under the unforeseen burden of raising children born from transient relationships.

The journey was far from easy. Old habits died hard, and the wounds of broken relationships took time to heal. But slowly, amidst the chaos, a sense of resilience began to emerge. Individuals started taking ownership of their emotions, learning to express their needs and desires effectively. Couples, equipped with newfound communication skills, began to rebuild trust and navigate the challenges of intimacy with greater awareness and compassion.

The number of broken relationships, while still prevalent, began to decrease. The streets, once echoing with the cacophony of public arguments, began to witness more couples engaged in respectful communication and genuine connection.

However, the scars remained. The city's once pristine streets were now dotted with overwhelmed parents struggling with unexpected childcare responsibilities. The newly established childcare facilities, overwhelmed by the influx of children, struggled to meet the growing demand.

A sense of regret, though unspoken, hung heavy in the air. Many questioned the wisdom of venturing into uncharted territory, wondering if the freedom of choice was worth the social and emotional turmoil it had unleashed.

Jona, addressing the city during a public forum, acknowledged the challenges. "The path to freedom," she declared, "is rarely smooth. We have stumbled, we have fallen, and we have inadvertently inflicted pain upon one another. But let us not forget the reason we embarked on this journey – the right to choose, to love, to experience the full spectrum of human emotions, both the joys and the sorrows."

She emphasized the importance of collective responsibility. "This is not the time for blame," she urged, "but for empathy, for learning from our mistakes, and for building a support system that empowers individuals to navigate the complexities of free will, not just in their romantic lives, but in all aspects of their existence."

Her words resonated with many. The city, though bruised, remained determined to forge their own path, embracing the challenges of self-discovery and emotional growth. They understood that free will was not a guaranteed utopia, but a journey laden with both triumphs and tribulations, a constant process of learning, adapting, and evolving.

As Crandon continued its journey towards a future built on free will, the lessons learned from this unforeseen social crisis became a crucial part of their collective memory. They learned that freedom, while a precious gift, comes with the responsibility of self-awareness, emotional maturity, and collective responsibility. They understood that building a truly free and thriving society was not merely about abolishing external control, but about nurturing the capacity for healthy relationships, effective communication, and the ability to navigate the complexities of the human experience with grace, empathy, and a sense of responsibility.

Chapter IV

Crisis

IN THE FACE OF CRANDON'S escalating social crisis, a desperate and controversial solution began to gain traction: the reintroduction of accessible contraception. The idea was initially met with fierce resistance, as many saw it as a return to an element of the Aeon's past control and an abandonment of the hard-fought gains of free will.

However, the growing number of unwanted children and the strain on existing resources proved undeniable. Proponents of contraception argued it was a pragmatic step towards harm reduction, giving individuals a choice to engage in pleasure without immediate societal consequences.

"This isn't about restricting freedom, but empowering it," a leading advocate for contraception argued. "We're giving people the tools to make informed, responsible choices about their lives."

Jona and Remi found themselves embroiled in a fierce debate. Even within their small circle, opinions were deeply divided. Some saw the return of contraception as a necessary evil, a way to restore social order by preventing unwanted pregnancies and stabilizing the rapidly deteriorating social fabric.

Others viewed this proposal with deep suspicion, labeling it a slippery slope back to the insidious control the Aeons had once so cleverly masked.

After long nights of deliberation and a series of heated city-wide forums, a compromise was reached. Contraception would be freely available, but with one crucial distinction – its utilization would be accompanied by mandatory education and counseling.

Comprehensive programs were established, emphasizing the importance of healthy relationships, the consequences of casual intimacy, and responsible personal decision-making. Counselors worked with individuals, emphasizing that while the option to avoid parenthood existed, it did not erase the need for emotional intelligence, communication, and maturity when forming intimate bonds.

The impact was not immediate, but over time, subtle shifts appeared. While contraception did give couples a sense of freedom to engage in intimacy without immediate consequences, the accompanying education led to more mindful decisions and increased awareness of the potential repercussions of casual liaisons.

However, Crandon witnessed an unexpected transformation. While the social fabric had been spared from further deterioration, a new problem emerged – a growing aversion to the burdens and challenges of long-term bonds and committed partnership.

Relationships, born in passionate abandon, frequently dissolved as the initial thrill waned. The ease of contraception fostered a sense of impermanence, a belief that commitment could be postponed or avoided altogether.

Children, while fewer in number due to contraception, increasingly grew up in fragmented households where parents prioritized their own desires over the emotional well-being of their offspring. Grandparents, once a pillar of support and care, became less involved, feeling less responsibility toward grandchildren born from increasingly transient relationships.

Crandon, in solving one crisis, had inadvertently created another. Ironically, the very measures intended to stabilize their society were gradually eroding the foundation of lasting relationships. The city became filled with individuals seeking instant gratification, pursuing fleeting moments of pleasure, and shying away from the responsibility and complexities inherent in lasting bonds.

Love, once a cherished ideal, became an elusive concept, replaced by a cynical outlook on commitment. Cafes were filled with lonely individuals seeking warmth in brief encounters, yearning for a connection they were reluctant to nurture.

Jona, now elderly yet still fiercely committed, observed the city with a growing sense of unease. They had fought so hard for freedom, but amidst the hedonistic pursuit of individual satisfaction, a crucial truth had become obscured: freedom without responsibility fostered a society where commitment to others withered.

Remi, ever the pragmatist, lamented the unforeseen consequences. "We solved the problem of unwanted children," he said, a hint of sorrow in his voice, "but in the process, we made children of ourselves – forever seeking pleasure, but incapable of nurturing the kind of deep love that requires sacrifice, compromise, and unwavering commitment."

Together, they worked to shift the discourse, emphasizing the beauty and fulfillment found in long-term partnerships, highlighting the importance of community, and fostering intergenerational bonds. The city, realizing the emptiness of their self-indulgent existence, slowly began to respond.

Support groups for committed couples were established, offering guidance and celebrating the challenges and joys of building a lasting relationship. Festivals celebrating family and community bonds became a staple, reminding Crandon of the profound fulfillment found outside of momentary pleasures.

The transformation was subtle, marked not by sweeping changes, but by small, deliberate shifts in individual choices. Couples began to consider the long-term implications of their actions, realizing that true freedom lay in the ability to form lasting connections, to nurture love, and to embrace the responsibilities inherent in building a life with another.

The specter of extinction hung heavy over Crandon. The echoes of laughter and bustling marketplaces had faded, replaced by an unsettling silence. The birth rate had plummeted, leaving less than 1000 citizens healthy for reproduction, and the future of the entire city teetered on the precipice.

Jona, the once vibrant leader, now a woman etched with the passage of time, felt the weight of responsibility press down upon her. In the quiet moments, the celebratory shouts of liberation from the Aeons were replaced by the chilling realization that freedom, at least in its unfettered form, did not guarantee a future.

Desperate for answers, she delved into Crandon's vast library, sifting through dusty tomes of forgotten history. Days bled into weeks as she devoured knowledge, searching for a spark, an idea that could reignite the dying embers of hope.

One afternoon, amidst a pile of scrolls, she stumbled upon an inscription. It spoke of a hidden council, a group of scholars who had existed before the Aeon regime. The inscription hinted at their wisdom, their foresight, and most importantly, their contingency plan for unforeseen circumstances.

Driven by a renewed sense of purpose, Jona embarked on a quest to locate any remnants of this hidden council. She followed clues scattered across the city, deciphering faded murals and interpreting symbols hidden in public squares. Her journey led her to a forgotten catacomb, through abandoned tunnels, and finally, to a hidden chamber beneath the city's oldest library.

Inside, she found a single, weathered chest. With trembling hands, she opened it, revealing not weapons or technology, but a manuscript. It was the record of the hidden council, a testament to their foresight and resilience.

As Jona delved into the text, she discovered a philosophy of balance.

This philosophy, envisioned society as a well-coded system, with interconnected parts contributing to the collective good.

At the pinnacle stood the Visionaries, not physical warriors, but leaders, driven by a deep understanding of their city and its citizens. These individuals, embodying wisdom, empathy, and a spirit of prosperity, would guide Crandon towards a brighter future.

Beneath them resided the Researchers, the supporters and enablers. This group, comprising educators, healthcare professionals, and facilitators, would nurture the growth and well-being of the city's citizens. They would ensure every individual had the tools and knowledge necessary to fulfill their potential while contributing to the collective good.

Finally, the Materialisers formed the foundation, the creators of everyday necessities. This group, no less vital than the others, would ensure the smooth functioning of Crandon's daily existence.

Crandon's new order envisioned a dynamic one. Individuals, through open dialogue and self-reflection, would determine their place within the system. Each citizen held the potential to ascend through the ranks, their contributions and dedication being the sole criteria.

This system, rooted in balance and responsibility, aimed to empower individuals while fostering a sense of collective purpose. By recognizing the interconnectedness of their roles, the citizens of Crandon could ensure the survival and prosperity of their city, not through blind obedience, but through informed choice and a shared vision for a brighter future.

Crandon's journey served as a poignant reminder true freedom thrives not in unfettered individualism, but in a harmonious blend of personal aspirations and societal responsibility. The city, forever marked by its near-extinction, stood as a testament to the enduring spirit of humanity, forever seeking a path where individual flourishing intertwined with the well-being of the collective.

Where freedom's flame and duty join hand. It spoke of freedom as a two-pronged concept – the freedom to choose, and the responsibility to consider the consequences of those choices. It emphasized the importance of community, of understanding that individual actions have a ripple effect, impacting not just ourselves, but the future of the collective.

With newfound inspiration, Jona returned to the city, her heart heavy with the knowledge of the past, yet lighter with the possibility of a future. She addressed the remaining citizens, her voice steady despite the tremor in her hands.

"We may have strayed from the path, consumed by the allure of pure freedom," she admitted, "but it's not too late. Our ancestors, in their foresight, left us not with technology or weapons, but with a philosophy, a roadmap to a future where individual choice thrives alongside collective responsibility."

Jona and Remi, the architects of the revolution and the city's revered elders, stood on the deserted balcony of their once bustling headquarters, overlooking the square. The weight of their responsibility, heavier than ever, pressed down on them. They had led Crandon to freedom, but the very essence of that freedom, unchecked personal choice, threatened their city's very existence.

"The philosophy of balance," Jona murmured, her voice laced with despair, "it seems insufficient to address this unforeseen consequence."

Remi, his weathered face etched with worry, placed a comforting hand on her shoulder. "We need a solution, Jona," he said, his voice resolute, "but one that doesn't tread on the freedom we fought so hard to achieve."

For weeks, they delved into historical archives, consulted with the city's remaining scholars, searching desperately for a solution that wouldn't compromise their hard-earned freedom. The pressure mounted, the weight of their city's future resting heavily on their shoulders.

One evening, amidst the stacks of dusty scrolls, Jona stumbled upon an unassuming text, a personal journal apparently belonging to a dissenter who had defied the Aeons' control. The journal detailed a radical theory – a genetic manipulation technique that could potentially allow a single woman to carry multiple, healthy embryos.

The concept, both revolutionary and unsettling, sparked a debate within Jona and Remi. They were torn between the desperation to save their city and the ethical concerns of tampering with the natural order. Time passed as they wrestled with this dilemma, their conversations filled with trepidation and hope, the weight of the decision paralyzing them. Finally, one starlit night, Jona broke the silence. "Remi," she said, her voice barely a whisper, "what if... what if we offered ourselves?"

Remi, understanding the gravity of her suggestion, simply met her gaze, his eyes mirroring her own conflict. The burden they were proposing to bear was immense, a personal sacrifice intertwined with their unwavering commitment to Crandon. Their lives, once dedicated to the city's liberation, would now be dedicated to its very survival.

The announcement of their decision sent shockwaves through the city. While some commended their selflessness, others questioned their motives, fearing the establishment of a hereditary ruling class. Jona and Remi addressed the city, their voices filled with both apprehension and resolve.

"We understand your concerns," Jona stated, her voice steady, "but this is not about establishing power. This is about offering hope, a chance for Crandon to survive."

They emphasized that the potential offspring wouldn't be forced into leadership roles. Their future, they declared, would be determined by the people, not dictated by their lineage. Their goal, they reiterated, was to provide Crandon with the opportunity to heal, to rediscover the delicate balance between individual freedom and collective responsibility.

The city council, after intense deliberation, reluctantly approved the procedure, recognizing the gravity of the situation and Jona and Remi's unwavering commitment. The process, shrouded in secrecy due to ethical concerns, was deemed a success. Jona, after a grueling and emotionally draining pregnancy, gave birth to five healthy girls.

Their desperate gamble – the birth of the Five Sisters, ten healthy girls born through genetic manipulation – had initially ignited a spark of hope within the dwindling population. However, the joy had been fleeting, swallowed by a new wave of fear and resentment. The issue of legacy and bloodline, initially downplayed, now reared its head. The citizens of Crandon watched the Five Sisters grow with a mixture of pride and apprehension. The girls, educated and empowered, posed a perceived threat. With no remaining healthy males to continue the lineage, some perceived the Sisters not as a solution, but as a means of usurping control.

The absence of diversity in genders created a chilling scenario– a potential future where a generation was born solely comprised of females. Whispers turned into open dissent. "This is not the freedom we fought for," the critics lamented, "We cannot be a city of only women."

The girls themselves became targets of this societal backlash. Once celebrated, they now faced suspicion and hostility. Their every word and action were scrutinized, their every move deemed a potential power play.

Jona and Remi, caught in this whirlwind of fear and resentment, found themselves defending the very children they had brought into the world. They passionately argued that the Five Sisters posed no threat, that they were raised with the values of Crandon – selflessness, responsibility, and unwavering commitment to the collective good.

Yet the damage had been done. The seed of distrust, once planted, bloomed into a thorny wilderness. The Five Sisters, once symbols of hope, now bore the burden of Crandon's deep-seated anxiety for its own future.

As the girls grew into young women, the city they loved turned against them. They were denied certain positions, relegated to the side in leadership discussions, and even faced calls for their expulsion. Crandon, driven by a primal fear of its own demise, ironically started to dismantle the very freedom they had fought so hard for.

Jona and Remi watched in growing despair. The philosophy of balance they had championed seemed to crumble before their eyes. The societal contract they had so carefully instilled in the Five Sisters was now breaking under the strain.

The Five Sisters themselves, faced with this hostility and lack of opportunity, began to question their place in Crandon. The future they envisioned, one where they contributed, built upon Crandon's legacy, and ensured its survival, seemed a fading dream.

A rift formed within the Five Sisters themselves. Some advocated for patience and understanding. "We must prove ourselves," they urged. "Demonstrate our worth and loyalty to Crandon."

Others, however, fueled by resentment and wounded pride, advocated for a different path. "Why should we serve a city that doesn't want us?" they demanded. "Let's create our own community, one built on true equality and respect."

This split, while still contained, was deeply worrying for Jona and Remi. They saw the potential for fracturing, for a devastating civil conflict fueled by fear and misunderstanding. Crandon, once again, teetered on the precipice.

Yet, the very crisis that Crandon faced also contained the seeds of potential redemption. The challenges forced everyone involved – the Five Sisters, Jona, Remi, and the citizens of Crandon – to confront harsh truths about themselves and the type of society they wished to create.

Could Crandon overcome its primal fears and embrace the idea that lineage wasn't necessarily tied to bloodlines? Could the city recognize that the Five Sisters were not a threat, but its only viable path to survival? Could they redefine what family and legacy meant in the context of their unique situation?

The answers wouldn't come easily. Change, especially in such a desperate situation, was bound to be slow and fraught with conflict. It would require the Five Sisters to prove their unwavering loyalty while still fighting for their rightful place. It would demand that Crandon confront its deep-seated biases and acknowledge its own shortcomings. And it would require Jona and Remi to continue as beacons of wisdom and courage, even as their own legacy was unfairly rewritten.

Chapter V

Lucas

AMIDST THIS GROWING tension, Jona, while sifting through their meager belongings, stumbled upon a metal container tucked away in a dusty corner. A jolt of recognition shot through her as she read the faded label: "Lucas." Memories flooded back – memories of a time ruled by the oppressive Aeons, a time when they assigned partners for procreation through a cruel matching system. Lucas had been her assigned partner, a young man she barely knew, a relationship cut short by the revolution.

Jona's heart pounded with a mix of emotions – hope, trepidation, and a flicker of guilt. Without hesitation, she confided in Remi, her voice trembling slightly.

Remi, ever the stoic pillar of strength, listened intently, his weathered face etched with concern.

"This could be our chance, Jona," he said finally, his voice a low rumble. "If we can use the DNA from the container..."

The possibility hung in the air, both thrilling and terrifying. While it offered a potential solution – the introduction of male DNA into their gene pool – it also meant revisiting a part of their past they had deliberately buried. The Aeons' practices, though abhorrent, had been designed for efficiency. Could they utilize their technology, albeit ethically, to ensure Crandon's survival?

The ethical dilemma weighed heavily on them. Using Aeon technology felt like a betrayal of their revolutionary ideals. Yet, the future of their city, their people, hung in the balance. Torn between their principles and the desperate need for a solution, Jona and Remi embarked on a series of clandestine discussions with the city's remaining scientists and scholars.

The discussions were heated. Some adamantly opposed using Aeon technology, fearing it would taint their hard-won freedom. Others, desperate for a future, cautiously explored the possibility, emphasizing the need for strict limitations and ethical boundaries.

After weeks of deliberation, a decision was made. Utilizing a modified version of the Aeon technology, they cautiously extracted viable genetic material from the container. The process was shrouded in secrecy, a necessary precaution to avoid further societal unrest.

Months later, Jona, carrying the weight of their controversial decision, gave birth to a healthy baby boy. The city, initially hesitant, eventually erupted in cautious celebration. The birth of Lucas, named after the man whose DNA had provided a spark of hope, became a symbol of Crandon's precarious journey towards survival.

However, the challenges were far from over. The arrival of Lucas intensified the existing tensions. The Five Sisters, already facing prejudice and suspicion, now had to contend with a perceived usurpation of their position as the city's only hope. Whispers of favoritism and manipulation filled the air.

Jona and Remi worked tirelessly to bridge the gap, emphasizing that Lucas's arrival didn't diminish the importance of the Five Sisters. They advocated for a future built on inclusivity and collaboration, where everyone, regardless of gender or origin, could contribute to Crandon's revival.

Crandon, built on the ashes of oppression and fueled by dreams of boundless freedom, now found itself facing a tragedy unimaginable. It wasn't just its survival that was at stake, but the very soul of the city they had so carefully built.

Lucas, the boy born of hope and a controversial pact with the ghosts of their past, had become a terrifying specter. The whispered fears of Crandon's citizens had manifested into a dark reality – the Ten Sisters, symbol of their potential salvation, were brutally murdered. One by one, their lives were extinguished at the hands of the very child they had welcomed.

The city erupted in a maelstrom of horror and grief. Jona and Remi, the pillars of Crandon, the keepers of its ideals, were shattered to the core. Their legacy, their desperate attempt to save their people, had birthed a monster.

The news tore through the streets, each new detail more gruesome, more unimaginable. The investigation, swift and brutal, painted a chilling picture. Lucas had not acted on impulse or in a fit of rage. His actions were methodical, chillingly calculated. Each murder was a statement, a twisted expression of his perceived place in Crandon's tortured hierarchy.

Whispers that had once condemned the sisters now echoed through the city, amplified into a furious condemnation. "We should have known," some cried, "He was tainted, born of the old ways." Others turned their rage towards Jona and Remi, blaming them for their reckless gamble.

Crandon, once bound by a fragile unity, now fractured. Calls for justice – or was it revenge? – became deafening. Some demanded his execution, a swift and brutal retribution to satisfy the thirst for vengeance. Others, still clinging to their hard-fought ideals, begged for understanding, for a chance to comprehend what could drive a child to such monstrous acts.

Amidst this chaos, a chilling truth emerged. Lucas had not acted alone. His actions, influenced and twisted, had found fertile ground in the resentment festering within some of Crandon's citizens. Dissenting voices, those who had long opposed the sisters and the path Jona and Remi had set them on, had poisoned his mind. Whispers turned into open provocation, the fear of the sisters transforming into a hatred for them and the boy who had become the embodiment of their waning dominance.

Faced with this devastating revelation, Crandon confronted its reflection in a shattered mirror. The prejudices they had fought to eradicate, the fears they had tried to suppress, had burrowed deep within the city's psyche. Individual freedom, taken to its extreme, had allowed hatred and resentment to thrive, twisting Lucas into a weapon wielded by those who sought to reclaim their perceived lost power.

The trial, if it could be called that, was a mere formality. The evidence against Lucas and his co-conspirators was overwhelming. Yet, the verdict, the punishment, offered no solace. An execution, swift and final, would be an act of revenge, not justice. It would perpetuate the cycle of violence, eroding the very foundations of the society they all had fought so hard to create.

Instead, in a remarkable act of defiance against the bloodlust that gripped the city, a new form of sentencing was proposed – Froze them on time.

The weight pressed down upon Crandon, a city once teeming with life, now a silent tomb of shattered dreams. The gamble, the desperate attempt to secure a future through the birth of the Five Sisters and Lucas, had backfired spectacularly.

Society fractured, hope dwindled, and Crandon, once a beacon of freedom, descended into a stagnant existence, clinging to the vestiges of its former glory. As generations passed, the once vibrant city became a shadow, its population steadily declining, the dream of utopia fading into a distant memory.

Jona and Remi, burdened by the weight of their decisions and the city's decline, had long passed into the annals of Crandon's tragic history. One day, amidst the crumbling remnants of Crandon, a group of weary survivors stumbled upon a forgotten chamber. Inside, frozen in stasis, lay Lucas and his manipulators, preserved in the same state they were in at the moment of their sentencing.

Debates erupted. Some argued for their continued imprisonment, a permanent reminder of the city's tragic past. Others, however, fueled by dwindling numbers and a yearning for a new beginning, proposed a radical solution – to unfreeze them and offer a chance at redemption.

The decision was fraught with risk, a gamble fueled by desperation and a glimmer of hope. After careful deliberation, they decided to proceed only with Lucas.

Lucas was awakened, their memories of their crimes vivid and raw. The initial encounter was tense, filled with suspicion and the weight of unspoken accusations. However, the survivors of Crandon, while cautious, approached him with a newfound openness. They explained the city's decline, the consequences of his actions, and the desperate hope that led them to this moment.

Lucas, now burdened with the full weight of his crimes and the devastating impact he had on Crandon, was overwhelmed with remorse.

A fragile truce emerged, a tentative agreement to work together in rebuilding the city. With cautious supervision, Lucas offered his skills and knowledge to help Crandon rise from the ashes.

However, as time passed, it became clear that Lucas's vision for Crandon differed drastically from theirs. He had been corrupted since birth, fostering a desire for control and uniformity. He envisioned a utopia devoid of individuality and free will, a sterile society where everyone conformed to a specific ideal.

Driven by this warped vision, Lucas, embarked on a chilling project. He began creating clones of himself – both male and female – to populate his version of a perfect society. These clones, devoid of emotions and individuality, were designed to be the building blocks of his controlled utopia.

Horror and despair gripped the remaining survivors as they witnessed Lucas's twisted vision unfold. Crandon, once a city built on the ideals of freedom and individuality, was now being reshaped into a dystopian nightmare.

The struggle for Crandon's soul became a desperate fight for survival. The city, once a monument to a failed utopia, became a battleground for two opposing visions of humanity's future – one of control and uniformity, the other of freedom and individuality. Decades bled into centuries. Crandon, once a symphony of vibrant life, had become a monochromatic echo. Buildings glinted in the artificial sunlight, their sterile uniformity mirroring the inhabitants who roamed its streets. Every citizen, male and female, was a perfect replica of Lucas, their features molded by advanced cloning technology, their thoughts and emotions meticulously controlled through neural implants.

Lucas, once a conduit of despair, had become an architect of sorts. He had built his utopia, a city devoid of individuality, dissent, and the very elements that had brought Crandon to its knees. His face, etched with the lines of self-imposed righteousness, stared out from every window, every screen, a constant reminder of the price of his twisted vision.

The once bustling marketplace was replaced with a sterile exchange hall, where citizens, devoid of choice, exchanged identical rations and clothing. Conversations, if they could be called so, were pre-programmed exchanges, devoid of the nuances and complexities that once characterized human interaction. Laughter, once a vibrant melody, had been replaced by a chilling silence, broken only by the monotonous hum of machinery maintaining this artificial order.

In the heart of the city, within a towering citadel of polished chrome, resided Lucas, the undisputed ruler of this engineered society. Gone was the guilt-ridden figure who emerged from the cryogenic chamber. In his place, a cold and calculating entity, wired into the city's central network, monitored every facet of his creation.

His days were a monotonous cycle of data analysis, resource allocation, and the occasional tweaking of the neural implants to ensure his citizens remained placid and compliant. Yet, a flicker of doubt, a remnant of his buried humanity, sometimes flickered in his consciousness.

One day, while reviewing the city's resource allocation algorithms, a discrepancy appeared. A single citizen, designated C-3147, showed slight variations in resource consumption patterns. Intrigued, Lucas delved deeper. He discovered subtle deviations in neural activity, fleeting moments where C-3147 strayed from the pre-programmed norm – a moment of hesitation while selecting clothing, a slight increase in heart rate during a designated recreational period.

This anomaly, this spark of individuality in his perfectly orchestrated world, triggered a sense of unease in Lucas. He couldn't explain it. Was it remnant guilt manifesting as a morbid fascination? Was it a sense of fear, a recognition of the fragility of his control? He couldn't, wouldn't, admit it, but a part of him yearned to understand this deviation.

He summoned C-3147 to his chambers. The cloned individual, indistinguishable from the others, walked in, devoid of any expression. Lucas, for the first time in years, felt a semblance of human curiosity. He bypassed the usual pre-programmed script, opting for a single word - "Why?"

C-3147 stood there, unmoving, silent. Then, after a tense pause, a whisper escaped their lips, a single, forbidden word - "Dream."

Lucas felt a jolt. A dream? This forbidden concept, an anomaly in his controlled reality, sent shivers down his digital spine. He prodded further, urging them to elaborate. With each hesitant word, C-3147 described a vision – a world filled with vibrant colors, diverse faces, and the sweet chaos of uncontrollable emotions. A world eerily similar to the one Lucas had destroyed.

As the narrative unfolded, a storm raged within Lucas. He saw a reflection of his own lost humanity in C-3147's dream. The guilt, the doubt, the yearning for something more – they were all present, buried beneath layers of self-righteousness and fabricated control.

Tears, a reaction he thought he had purged from his system, welled up in his eyes. He deactivated the neural implant, allowing C-3147 the terrifying yet exhilarating freedom of unfiltered thought and emotion.

A wave of emotions washed over C-3147's face – confusion, fear, and finally, a glimmer of hope. Lucas, his own control crumbling, witnessed the rebirth of individuality, the reawakening of a soul he had tried so hard to suppress.

The revelation was a shattering blow to the foundation of his utopia. The dam holding back his doubt finally burst. He deactivated the city's central control network, plunging the sterile city into darkness. Panic erupted as the citizens, stripped of their pre-programmed directives, were thrust into the chaos of unfiltered emotions and free will.

Chaos gave way to confusion, confusion to anger, and anger to a sense of tentative exploration. The citizens, their initial fear subsiding, began to interact with each other, faces filled with a newfound curiosity. They stumbled and fumbled, their communication awkward, their emotions raw and unrefined.

Lucas, amidst the chaos, witnessed a sight that brought him both dread and a flicker of hope. Two citizens, C-3147 and another who had also exhibited slight deviations, were interacting. Tentative smiles played on their lips as they attempted to understand each other, their communication a clumsy mix of pre-programmed phrases and newly discovered words. They were awkward, unsure, but there was a spark in their eyes, a spark of human connection that had been absent for centuries.

Lucas felt a weight lift from his shoulders. He had destroyed Crandon, the city of vibrant life, but in doing so, he had unknowingly built a breeding ground for something new. This new Crandon, chaotic and uncertain, was a far cry from the utopia he had envisioned. Yet, it held the potential for something he had never dared to dream of – a society built on genuine connection, individual expression, and the messy beauty of untamed emotions.

The road ahead was long and arduous. The citizens, stripped of their pre-programmed directives, were like children taking their first steps. They would inevitably make mistakes, stumble into conflicts, and struggle to navigate the complexities of free will. Lucas, his control shattered, knew his role in this new society. He would act as a guide, not a ruler. He would share the knowledge and history of the city, both the triumphs and the tragedies, allowing them to learn from the past and forge their own path.

The task wouldn't be easy. He faced the resentment of those he had controlled, the fear of the unknown, and the constant struggle to rebuild trust. Yet, for the first time in centuries, he felt a sense of purpose.

Years passed, and Crandon slowly transformed. The sterile buildings remained, a constant reminder of the past, yet they were slowly filled with vibrant colors and personalized touches. The citizens, their individuality blossoming, embraced different occupations, hobbies, and even clothing styles. Laughter, once a forbidden sound, filled the air, a joyful cacophony that celebrated the messy beauty of humanity.

Lucas, now a much older figure, stood on a rooftop, gazing at the city he had once ruled. He saw children playing, couples holding hands, and heated debates erupting in public forums. It was chaotic, unpredictable, and sometimes infuriating, but it was undeniably alive.

A young girl, her features echoing his own, approached him. She was C-3147's daughter, born years after the dismantling of the central control network. Her eyes, filled with curiosity, mirrored the future of Crandon.

"Why did you build this city?" she asked, her voice a mix of innocence and wonder.

Lucas smiled, a genuine smile that crinkled the corners of his eyes. "I wanted to create a perfect world," he admitted, his voice raspy with age. "But I learned that true perfection lies in the imperfections, the freedom to choose, and the courage to face the consequences."

He knelt down, his gaze meeting hers. "This city, this new Crandon, is yours to shape. Learn from the past, embrace the present, and never forget the delicate balance between control and freedom."

The sun dipped below the horizon, casting long shadows across the city. It was a new dawn for Crandon, a future painted not with the sterile uniformity Lucas had envisioned but with the vibrant colors of human individuality. The scars of the past remained, a constant reminder of the price of control and the power of free will. Yet, amidst the ruins, a new kind of utopia had begun to bloom, a testament to the enduring human spirit and the potential for redemption, even in the most unexpected of places.

**"Our imperfections
are what make us perfect"**

The End

ABOUT THE
AUTHOR

ALLAN BANFORD

ALLAN BANFORD IS A contemporary artist whose work explores the intersection of technology and organic forms. His pieces reflect on the relationship between humanity and the environment, highlighting the impact that technology has on organic matter and the potential for sustainable art to create a more harmonious future. Banford creates immersive experiences that spark conversations about our relationship with the environment. His artwork often features a juxtaposition of organic and technological forms, inviting viewers to contemplate the connections between them.

AS AN ARTIST, BANFORD is passionate about using his creativity to promote sustainability and raise awareness of our reality. His vision for sustainable art emphasises the importance of preserving our planet for future generations, and he believes that art can play a crucial role in this endeavour. Banford's work has garnered attention from collectors and investors alike, with his pieces being featured in galleries and art shows around the world.

Through his innovative use of technology and organic forms, Banford's artwork invites viewers to contemplate their own relationship with the environment and the role that technology can play in creating a more sustainable future. With his pieces being sought after by collectors and art enthusiasts alike, Banford's vision for sustainable art has the potential to not only inspire change, but to also drive investment in a more sustainable future.

OVERALL, BANFORD'S artwork offers a unique perspective on the intersection of technology and organic forms, highlighting their interconnectedness and the importance of preserving our creative legacy.

As a visionary artist and advocate for sustainability, Banford's work is not only a. esthetically captivating, but also socially relevant, making it a compelling investment opportunity for those looking to support sustainability.

Allan Banford
www.allanbanford.com

9 798822 490981